Clark Jillson

Address on New Hampshire and Vermont

Clark Jillson

Address on New Hampshire and Vermont

ISBN/EAN: 9783741123412

Manufactured in Europe, USA, Canada, Australia, Japa

Cover: Foto ©Andreas Hilbeck / pixelio.de

Manufactured and distributed by brebook publishing software
(www.brebook.com)

Clark Jillson

Address on New Hampshire and Vermont

ADDRESS

ON

NEW HAMPSHIRE

AND

VERMONT:

THEIR UNIONS,
SECESSIONS AND DISUNIONS.

DELIVERED BEFORE
The New Hampshire Antiquarian Society,
JULY 15, 1879.

By CLARK JILLSON.

WORCESTER :
PRESS OF CLARK JILLSON.
1882.

ADDRESS.

WE STAND before the hours, crowded to the front and into the future by the lapse of time. The last decade has taken its position behind us, and the generations have thus been carried to a point one hundred years beyond the grand historic period of the Western Empire.

One hundred years ago this very hour, "Mad Anthony Wayne," the hero of Stony Point, was marshalling his troops for that memorable assault; and when he was wounded, the thrilling order he gave, "March on; carry me into the fort, and let me die at the head of the column," together with the account of the intrepid manner in which Col. Fleury struck the British standard with his own hand, and the words of Major Posey, "The Fort's our own," ran beyond the lines and through the Colonies like the echoes of inspiration. But the full account of this tragic event has not been preserved by tradition alone. Unlike hundreds of other remarkable occurrences during the revolutionary period, it found its way into written history, and is now known as one of the most daring exploits of the war.

Tradition is too fickle for practical use, always taking from or adding to the real fact; and what we thus gather in relation to any past event is only worthy to be called a story, unless it can be traced to some well authenticated record, made at or about the time it occurred. The nearer worthless we can make tradition in its application to the future, the more complete will be the knowledge of coming generations in relation to what is now transpiring; and among the many duties we are under obligations to perform, that of making and preserving authentic history is one of the most important and imperative. The neglect of such duty by one man, may, in time to come, involve a nation in doubt, and make future generations busy with unsatisfactory research for hundreds of years. Against such omissions the world has been struggling through all the historic past; and while I speak to-day there are hundreds of men in New England engaged in experimental labor upon which they are employing the best mental efforts of their life's prime, unconscious of the fact that they are spending their time on the hundredth edition of the same work.

More than half of our inventors are now studying upon what has been or will be rejected matter, for the reason that they have no adequate facilities for finding out what other minds have accomplished, hence the same thing will be invented over and over again without any perceptible change, even of form.

It has been claimed by some that too much is already being written and printed; and when the recent proposition for an enlargement of the rooms containing the Congressional Library at Washington was being discussed, a certain newspaper in Massachusetts advocated burning the books in preference to furnishing more room! It is true that worthless books, so called, are not extremely rare, and yet it requires a sublime stupidity to make a book of no present or future value. The solitary fact that a book has been printed is worthy of preservation. If it contains but a single word bearing a new relation to any other, it ought to be preserved; and the man who advocates the burning of books would be inconsistent in opposing his own cremation.

Things of little apparent consequence to-day are liable to become famous to-morrow, and after it is too late comes the struggle for a knowledge of their early history.

When Christopher Columbus was wandering over the countries of Europe, begging for royal patronage to assist in carrying forward an enterprise that existed only in his own brain, in the form of a vision, there appeared no friendly hand to record his pleadings. It was considered enough for posterity to know that he had been refused and placed on the beggar's list. When he finally succeeded in presenting his claim to the Court of Spain, it was referred to a commission who reported after a delay of about seven years, that the project of Columbus was "vain and impossible." Had all his plans been thus defeated, the discovery of the new world might have been delayed for a century. It was then that the destinies of America hung in a balance.

The manner in which Columbus presented his cause to the commissioners is unknown. The history of their deliberations within the decorated walls and under the frescoed arches of the Alhambra, where the future of a great Republic was dimly outlined four hundred years ago, has not been written. The original plan of his then intended voyage toward the setting sun has been lost. The words he uttered to the Queen on his return to Granada, in obedience to her summons, after he had been refused a further hearing by Ferdinand, at which time she pledged to him the jewels of her own crown of Castile, were known only to her and to him, and considered unworthy of record; but the corner stone of an empire, now one of the great powers of earth, was then and there laid.

Doctor Franklin, with all his sagacity and foresight, did not comprehend the importance of his own rude experiments with electricity, nor even dream that the thread connecting his door key with a kite, was in the least degree suggestive of the iron cord yet to span the globe from continent to continent, passing under the sea, transmitting its pulsations of thought around the world.

When Capt. Samuel Morey was experimenting

with his newly invented Steamboat upon the waters
of New Hampshire and Vermont, in 1792, he evidently did not comprehend that the culmination of
his thought, wrought out and perfected by other
hands, would at some future time revolutionize the
commerce of all the nations on the earth.

Those three young men who assembled in the
town of Hopkinton, N. H., on the 19th day of Nov.,
1859, and organized themselves into the Philo-
mathic Club, which they resolved should never
contain more than seven members, nor cease to exist except by the unanimous consent of the last one
living, may well be reminded that

"Tall oaks from little acorns grow,"

and that the creed of a modern prophet needs fre-
quent revision. Out of that humble beginning has
sprung your Society, with its rare and valuable
library, its extensive collection of relics and curiosi-
ties. Through its influence persons of similar tastes
have been brought together, and their efforts combined in a common cause for the public good; and
you are now making history from year to year
about which there will be no dispute or misunder-
standing in the future. You have been so fortunate
as to preserve a record of your early work, and posterity will thank you for handing it down to them.

I have thus called your attention to these several
cases for the purpose of intimating that any important historical event, growing out of a multitude of

minor unrecorded occurrences, cannot easily be traced to any well defined cause.

Nearly all historical matter relating to the early settlement of New England is of such a general character as to make it next to impossible to give a connected account of any important event without taxing the imagination to supply some of its details. The little incidents that go to make up a symmetrical statement have generally been lost by reason of the failure to make their record at the time they occurred, and the whole transaction, presented in general terms, is often vague, uninteresting, and not easily comprehended.

The controversy between New York and New Hampshire in relation to the territory now known as Vermont, covering a period of about forty years, has come down to us in a great measure through the uncertain channels of tradition; but there has been enough preserved and authenticated from which to present a general view of the main transactions during that eventful period. The lesser details constituting the cause of this long and bitter contest, were evidently so numerous and obscure, passing so rapidly without being recorded, as to make the statement of an aggregate made up from them exceedingly difficult, and render conclusions drawn therefrom vague and uncertain. Upon looking over the field with some care, I am obliged to conclude that each and every person who makes an investigation of this subject will be obliged to attribute the result to such causes as his judgment shall dictate, from the few facts that have been preserved in history.

In treating the subject under consideration, I am obliged to omit any detailed statement relating to the condition of New Hampshire in early times.

The civil and ecclesiastical difficulties of the three governments of Dover, Exeter and Portsmouth—their union with Massachusetts in 1642—their separation in 1680, and their organization as a government with John Cutt for President—the subsequent administrations of Walter Barefoot and Edward Cranfield—their reunion with Massachusetts in 1686 under the presidency of Joseph Dudley, of Edmund Andros in 1687, of Simon Bradstreet in 1689—their return to a separate government in 1692, in which position they remained for a period of ten years, under Usher, Partridge and Allen—the re-appointment of Dudley, and their third union with Massachusetts in 1702, and from that time up to the advent of Benning Wentworth in 1741—must be passed over without further remark.

On the third day of July, 1741, Benning Wentworth was made Governor of the Province of New Hampshire, the southern boundary of which was by a line running paralel with the Merrimack River, three miles north thereof, till it reached a point due north of Pawtucket Falls; thence by a straight line due west "until it meets with his majesty's other governments." This language was construed by

Governor Wentworth to mean that the southerly line of New Hampshire extended as far west as that of the two Charter governments, Connecticut and Massachusetts Bay, each of which had exercised jurisdiction to within twenty miles of Hudson's River. By this appointment the union between New Hampshire and Massachusetts was again dissolved, and each Colony was left under the shadow of its own destiny.

On the 17th day of November, 1749, Governor Wentworth addressed a letter to Governor Clinton of New York, for the purpose of giving notice that he proposed to issue grants covering territory west of the Connecticut River; and also asking his excellency to state how far north of Albany the Government of New York extended by his Majesty's commissions, and how many miles to the eastward of Hudson's River. This letter was presented by Governor Clinton to the Council of New York, and thereupon the following order was adopted:

In Council New York 3d April 1750.

Ordered, That his Excellency do acquaint Governor Wentworth that this Province is bounded eastward by Connecticut River, the Letters Patent from King Charles the second to the Duke of York expressly granting all the lands from the west side of Connecticut River to the east side of Delaware Bay.

Before a copy of this order reached Governor Wentworth he had granted one township, six miles square, twenty-four miles easterly from Albany, and six miles north of Massachusetts line, presuming that New Hampshire was bounded by the same north and south line as Connecticut and Massachusetts Bay.

It will be seen that here was ample room for strife, as the Governor of New Hampshire had put the seal of his jurisdiction upon territory 40 miles west of where the Council of New York had declared the line between the two governments to be; and he had also paid deference to his own name by calling the newly granted township Bennington.

After some correspondence the two governors agreed to make a representation of the whole matter in dispute to his Majesty, which agreement was confirmed by his Majesty's Councils on the part of both governments. Richard Bradley Esq., Attorney General of New York, to whom the matter had been referred, gave an elaborate written opinion, wherein he recited the provisions of the Charter of Massachusetts Bay, and concluded by affirming that Connecticut River was the eastern boundary of the Colony of New York. Whoever throws away time enough to read the Attorney General's statement will surely discover in it a few weak points. The Surveyor General came to the rescue, and made certain suggestions which he thought proper to have added to the Attorney General's report. The Solicitor General made some discoveries, claiming that 10,000 acres of land, situated on the west side of Connecticut River which had been purchased by private persons from the government of Connecticut,

the same being lands laid out by the government of
Massachusetts Bay and exchanged for other lands
held by Connecticut, had become a part of New
Hampshire.

On the 28th day of December, 1763, Lieut. Gov.
Colden issued a proclamation in accordance with
the Attorney General's report, wherein he enjoined
the High Sheriff of the county of Albany to return
to him the names of all persons holding possession
of any lands west of Connecticut River, under the
grants of the government of New Hampshire, so that
they might be proceeded against according to law.
On the 13th day of March, 1764, Gov. Wentworth
issued a proclamation in answer to that of Lieut.
Gov. Colden, wherein he claimed that the Patent to
the Duke of York was obsolete, and commanded all
civil officers within his province, and all the inhabitants thereof to exercise jurisdiction as far westward
as his grants had been made, and to deal with all
persons who might presume to interrupt, "as law
and justice doth appertain, notwithstanding the pre-
tended right of jurisdiction mentioned in the proclamation" of Lieut. Gov. Colden.

The inhabitants occupying the territory over
which Gov. Wentworth proposed to exercise jurisdiction were not of one opinion in relation to the
rights claimed by New York and New Hampshire
respectively; and there was considerable feeling
manifest on both sides. The decision of this matter,

therefore, was to be one that would not be sanctioned by all parties, perhaps not by a majority.

The north and south line between New Hampshire and what was claimed to be New York, as established by the original grant to John Mason, commenced at a point on the line between New Hampshire and Massachusetts, sixty miles from the sea, which left quite an extensive territory between that and Connecticut River. If the decision should be in favor of Gov. Wentworth, some might claim that New Hampshire ought not to exercise its jurisdiction over the lands easterly from the river and westerly from the line defined by the grant to Mason. If the decision should be in favor of New York this same tract of land would still be left as a bone of contention, and the inhabitants of the territory in dispute might desire to divide, the easterly half going over to New Hampshire, and the westerly to New York, or the whole might unite and form a new State.

With all these contingencies pending, the application had been made, and great anxiety was felt in relation to the result. Governor Wentworth had issued one hundred and thirty-eight grants, and a large number, in some cases covering the same territory, had been granted to New York.

At the court of St. James, on the 20th day of July, 1764, it was declared that "the western banks of the river Connecticut, from where it enters the Province of Massachusetts Bay, as far North as the forty-fifth degree of North Latitude, to be the boundary line between New Hampshire and New York." This decision was not very objectionable to the government of New Hampshire or its people outside of the New Hampshire grants, it being considered only a change of jurisdiction; and if the land titles had been left undisturbed there would have been no further controversy between New Hampshire and New York.

But when the authorities of New York decided that the New Hampshire grants were null and always had been, and that the settlers would be compelled to re-purchase their lands or be ejected therefrom, a spirit of resentment arose among the pioneer settlers of the New Hampshire grants that could not be allayed short of revolution. The magnificent blunder of Charles the second in granting to the Duke of York, in 1664, all the lands from the west side of Connecticut River to the east side of Delaware Bay, without any reference to the charter of Massachusetts Bay, granted in 1620, or that of Connecticut granted in 1662, became apparent to the settlers, and they were led to question the validity of the grant under which the New York officials were beginning to proceed against them.

Within a month from the time of the passage of the royal decree establishing the eastern boundary of New York, Sheriff Schuyler found it necessary to appeal to the Commander-in-chief in a case where he claimed that a citizen of "Hoseck" had been ejected from his lands and tenements, and compelled

to suffer other wrongs at the hands of the New
Hampshire people. In consequence of this, the said
Sheriff arrested four persons and committed them to
jail in Albany. This was the New York version;
but Gov. Wentworth in his letter to Lieut. Gov.
Colden, claimed that "several of the inhabitants of
Pownal, at a time when the Deputy Sheriff was executing a legal precept, were set upon by the Sheriff of Albany and more than thirty armed men on
horseback, and that the Deputy Sheriff with the
three other principal inhabitants, were seized upon
and carried to Albany, where they were immedi-
ately committed to jail."

Whatever might have been the original provoca-
tion in this case, whether trifling or otherwise, an
effort was made, probably on both sides, to adjust it
by resorting to violence. False imprisonment together with the "Beech Seal" were frequently appealed to in the settlement of similar cases.

But at this period there were two parties residing
upon the territory now Vermont, one being favorable to New York and the other an ally of New
Hampshire, without any marked opposition to each
other; but none of them knew or cared for any law
except the individual code, dictated by individual
conscience; and never was a community better organized for a reign of terror than were these dis-
contented pioneers.

For the better administration of justice, and the
convenience of the settlers, three petitions were

presented to Lieut. Gov. Colden, in 1765, praying
that several counties might be erected covering territory occupied by the New Hampshire grants. One
of these petitions represented that one murder had
been committed "and one man more missing, that
is supposed to be murdered by the same Villin, and
that unless there be a county made as prayed for,
instead of good wholesome Inhabitants comeing and
Settling amongst us, the land will be filled with
nothing, but Villins and Murderers."

These petitions were read in council and referred
to a committee who reported on the twenty-second
day of October, 1765, that the inhabitants had "as
yet only an Equitable Title to the lands they pos-
sess; are utterly unacquainted with the laws of the
Province, and the modes of dispensing Justice therein," and recommended the appointment of "a number of fit persons for the conservation of the Peace
and the administration of Justice."

This was not a very flattering state of affairs to
be contemplated by those who had bought and paid
for their lands; nor was it much of a compliment
to the men fresh from Massachusetts and Connecticut, to be told that they were incapable of self
government.

Four counties were established and the "fit persons" appointed, but submission to their dictation
was never made complete. The settlers finally
concluded to resist the authority of New York, and
Samuel Robinson of Bennington was appointed to

represent them at the court of Great Britain and obtain, if possible, a confirmation of the New Hampshire grants, and his Majesty was induced to issue a special order for the purpose of prohibiting the Governor of New York from making future grants till his Majesty could further consider the whole matter.

No heed was paid to this order, but further grants were made, and fresh writs of ejectment were constantly being issued. Up to this time, and still later, most of the controversy had been carried on by persons residing west of the Green Mountains.

About this time a convention was held at Bennington wherein the delegates resolved to maintain their rights under the New Hampshire grants *by force.* Thereupon a military association was organized, with Ethan Allen for commander. The militia were called out by the Governor of New York to assist the Sheriff, but their sympathy seemed to be with the people to such an extent as to destroy all dicipline, and the appearance of Allen's troops caused them to disband. The next official display was in the form of a proclamation, issued by the Governor of New York, offering a reward of £150 for the arrest of Ethan Allen, and £50 each for Seth Warner and several others. On the other hand a proclamation was issued offering £5 for the Attorney General of the Colony of New York.

In 1772, the Governor of New York made an attempt to settle the controversy, and for that purpose opened correspondence with the Rev. Mr. Dewey of Bennington, and some others, signifying his willingness to confer with any person or persons the opposite party might choose, except Allen, Warner and three others. Capt. Stephen Fay and Mr. Jarius Fay were appointed to confer with the Governor; but this attempt at diplomacy failed for the reason that the Green Mountain Boys undertook to try their hand at the ejectment process while these negotiations were pending, which resulted in the abandonment of the whole scheme.

In the mean time the hostile condition of those occupying the New Hampshire grants became more and more alarming. Committees of safety were appointed in the several towns, and they were in constant communication for the purpose of devising the best means of common defence. The inhabitants were forbidden the acceptance of the honors of office under the Colony fo New York, on the pain of being "viewed." These "views" generally resulted in a liberal application of the "beech seal," vigorously laid upon the naked backs of the "yorkers."

The inhabitants of the "grants" were peculiar in many respects. Their laws, their manner of trial, their penalties and methods of punishment, were all vested in the Committee of Safety, and no person was allowed to escape on technicalities. Benjamin Hough was one of the King's Justices, under the authority of New York, and undertook to act in that capacity within the limits of the New Hampshire grants. He was brought before the Committee at

Sunderland, where he pleaded the jurisdiction of New York; but the Green Mountain Boys considered the decree of the convention, forbidding all persons from holding office, civil or military, under the Colony of New York, to be supreme, and passed the following sentence, which they proceeded to execute without giving time for spiritual advice or repentance:

"That the prisoner be taken from the bar of this committee of safety and be tied to a tree, and there, on his naked back, to receive one hundred stripes; his back being dressed, he should depart out of the the district, and on return, to suffer death, unless by special leave of the committee."

In another case, a person who had advised the settlers to submit to the authority of New York, after disregarding the warning of the committee, was arrested and carried to the Green Mountain Tavern in Bennington, where his defence was patiently heard, and then he was ordered "to be tied in an arm chair and hoisted to the sign, and there to hang two hours in sight of the people, as a punishment merited by his enmity to the rights and liberties of the inhabitants of the New Hampshire Grants."

The sign to which he was raised consisted of a post twenty-five feet high, with a sign-board at the top, upon which stood a stuffed catamount's skin facing New York, with a ferocious countenance. This Inn was ever after known as "Catamount Tavern" and was standing in 1869, but has since been destroyed by fire. Near this spot David Redding was hanged, June 1777, for "inimical conduct."

The General Assembly of New York, on the 5th day of February, 1774, passed resolutions wherein they called the Green Mountain Boys "the Bennington Mob," and recommended the passage of a law for their suppression and punishment. These proceedings made it necessary to call a general meeting of all the committees, which meeting was held at a private house in Manchester, on the 1st day of March, 1774. At this meeting the inhabitants resolved that while they were willing to encourage the execution of the laws, both civil and criminal, "that were so indeed," and that they should act only on the defensive, they would stand by and defend their friends and neighbors "at the expense of their lives and fortunes."

On the 9th day of March, 1774, the Assembly of New York passed an act that struck the key note of rebellion. It provided that if any person should oppose any civil officer of New York, in the discharge of his duty, or wilfully distroy the grain, corn or hay of any other person, being in any enclosure; or if any persons should assemble together, to the disturbance of the public peace, and demolish or pull down any building in the county of Albany or Charlotte, said offence should be deemed a felony, without benefit of clergy, and that the offender should suffer death. All crimes committed on the Grants were to be tried by the courts of Albany, and said courts were empowered to award execution against such as should be indicted for capital offences, who should not surrender themselves, in the same manner as if they had been convicted on a fair and impartial trial; and a reward of £50 each was offered for the arrest of Ethan Allen, Seth Warner, and six others.

On the 26th day of April, 1774, Ethan Allen and six others made and signed a remonstrance, wherein they resolved to inflict immediate death on whoever might attempt to apprehend any person indicted as a rioter for the purpose of inflicting the death penalty, declaring that "Our lives, liberties and properties are as verily precious to us as to any of the king's subjects; but if the governmental authority of New York insists upon killing us to take possession of our vineyards, let them come on; we are ready for a game of scalping with them, for our martial spirits glow with bitter indignation and consummate fury, to blast their infernal projects." About this time an attempt was made by Col. Philip Skeene to erect the New Hampshire Grants into a separate government under Great Britain; and it is said that his plan met with some favor on the part of the British government, and was probably instrumental in causing the Grants to declare themselves free and independent, in 1777.

Early in 1775 hostilities commenced between the Colonies and Great Britain, which overshadowed the controversy with New York, and the proscribed patriots of the New Hampshire Grants, with a bounty upon their heads, entered into the conflict with no fear or expectation of defeat; and on the tenth of May Ticonderoga and Crown Point were captured by Allen and Arnold.

It has generally been claimed that the first blood shed in the American Revolution, was at lexington, Mass., April 19th, 1775; but Lexington has a rival. The first conflict between the constituted authorities of Great Britain and the American Colonies occurred on the New Hampshire Grants, and was followed up by successive engagements between the loyalists and the rebels till the close of the revolution.

On the 5th day of September, 1774, Congress advised the people of the Colonies to maintain their liberties in such ways as should be found necessary; and the inhabitants of Cumberland county, for the purpose of resisting British tyranny and oppression, found it necessary to interfere with the holding of the court at Westminster, on the 13th day of March, 1775. On this occasion there was a desperate struggle on one side to maintain the authority of the British government, while on the other the liberties of the people were defended; and the lines between the two contending parties were as distinctly drawn and understood as at any future time during the war. Firearms were used, one man killed, several wounded, and many taken prisoners.

The battle of Lexington was fought within forty days from this time, and that of Bunker Hill within sixty days thereafter, against the same authority

and in the same cause. Had the war between the
Colonies and Great Britain been commenced when
the conflict occurred at Westminster? If so, the
first blood shed in the American Revolution was
within the jurisdiction of the New Hampshire Grants
and previous to the battle of Lexington.

Patrick Henry, after the fight at Westminster and
before that of Lexington, made the following statement which has never been disputed: "The war is
actually begun! The next gale that sweeps from
from the north, will bring to our ears the clash of
resounding arms! Our brethren are already in the
field! Why stand we here idle?"

The fight at Westminster was not a mob or a riot
any more than was that of Lexington, but a deliber-
ate resistance on the part of the people, to the government of Great Britain, and the first attempt to
defy, by an armed force, the authority of British
rule. If the Revolution was brought on by reason
of the defiance of laws made for the government of
the Colonies, and a resistance to their execution by
an armed force, we may justly claim that among the
wilds of the New Hampshire Grants was shed the
first blood in behalf of American liberty.

From this time for nearly two years the inhabitants of the Grants were active in their opposition to
British authority; and on the 15th day of January,
1777, at a convention held in Westminster, they
declared themselves to be "a separate, free and independent jurisdiction or State; by the name and for-

ever hereafter to be called, known and distinguished by the name of New Connecticut." On the 4th day of June, 1777, at a convention held in Windsor the name thus deliberately and formally given was abandoned, and the name of Vermont substituted. The reason given for making this change was, that a district of land on the Susquehanna river had been named New Connecticut, and it was claimed to be inconsistent for two districts on this continent to bear the same name.

This brief but decisive Declaration of Independence opened a new field for strife. The New York people were alarmed at the conduct of Vermont, and their committee of safety appealed to Congress, declaring it to be necessary that the commission of Col. Warner, who had been authorized to raise a regiment, be recalled; that nothing else would do justice to New York. Certain persons of ability and influence were urging Vermont to maintain her independence, choose delegates to Congress, and form a State Constitution. One Thomas Young printed and issued an address to the inhabitants of Vermont, urging them to be firm in their attempt to maintain the position they had assumed, assuring them that they had a right to choose how and by whom they should be governed. This address and other publications of a like nature were printed at Philadelphia, and the authorities of New York were much disturbed by their appearance.

One of the New York delegates presented the printed letter of Thomas Young to Congress on the 23d day of June, 1777. The entire subject was examined and discussed in committee of the whole, and on the 30th day of June resolutions were adopted declaring "That the independent government attempted to be established by the people styling themselves inhabitants of the New Hampshire Grants, can derive no countenance or justification from the act of Congress declaring the United Colonies to be independent of the crown of Great Britain, nor from any other act or resolution of Congress; and that the petition of Jonas Fay, Thomas Chittenden, Hiram Allen and Reuben Jones, praying that the district they represented might be ranked among the free and independent States, be dismissed." Although this action was favorable to New York, the Vermonters were still more confirmed in their determination to maintain their independence, if need be, against the whole world.

Up to this time there had been no controversy between Vermont and New Hampshire. In fact New Hampshire had acknowledged the independence of Vermont through her President, Mr. Weare, in a letter to Ira Allen, Secretary of the State of Vermont, wherein the New Hampshire Grants were designated as "a free and sovereign, but new State."

By the use of this language it was supposed that New Hampshire would use her influence to have Vermont recognized by Congress as an independent

State; but there was really no tenable ground for such a supposition. While it was understood that the easterly line of New York was by the Connecticut river, New Hampshire had no cause for complaint against Vermont for maintaining the same boundary The inhabitants on the east side of the river well knew that the east line of New York might have been extended to within sixty miles of the sea with as much propriety as any of the lands more than twenty miles east of Hudson's river could be claimed by the government of New York. The inhabitants of Vermont were also aware that the unchartered territory between the river and the Province of New Hampshire, as granted to John Mason, did not belong to New Hampshire with any more certainty than did the territory west of the river; and it was claimed that their declaration took effect on both sides of the river to such an extent that all persons residing west of the Mason line and east of the river, were free to join such government as they might desire, but more especially Vermont. These ideas were undoubtedly concocted and promulgated by the inhabitants west of the river and east of the Green Mountains, for the purpose of giving political strength to eastern Vermont, without any malicious intent to injure New Hampshire. The action taken on the part of the towns east of the river was remarkable.

On the 12th of March, 1778, sixteen towns east of Connecticut river declared in convention that they were not connected with any State, and thereupon petitioned the State of Vermont for an opportunity to confederate with its inhabitants. This petition was presented to the Assembly of Vermont. The members from the west side of the mountains, as might have been expected, were strongly opposed to it, but those from the vicinity of Connecticut river generally favored the union, and were so persistent in their efforts to accomplish the object of their strife as to propose a withdrawal from Vermont and the erection of a new State, including territory on both sides of the river. The independence of Vermont so recently and so unanimously promulgated to the world was now threatened with early dissolution; but it was found that a majority of the Assembly were not in favor of the annexation of any of the New Hampshire towns. This state of affairs caused some delay; and when the matter was brought before the next meeting of the Assembly, it was asserted that the inhabitants of the towns applying for annexation were nearly or quite unanimous, and that the state of New Hampshire would make no opposition. By means of these false representations, made by interested parties in both states, a vote of 37 to 12 was obtained in favor of the union; and by resolution it was provided that any town east of Connecticut river might be admitted on sending a representative to the Assembly of Vermont.

This attempt to swallow up New Hampshire created dissatisfaction and alarm among the inhabitants. An appeal was made to the Governor of Vermont, and a minority of the sixteen seceding towns claimed protection from the state of New Hampshire. An effort was made to interest Congress in their behalf. Col. Ethan Allen, who had been sent to Philadelphia for the purpose of solving this difficult problem, reported that Congress would not favor the union, but, in case it was abandoned, would not oppose the independence of Vermont.

In October, 1778, representatives from ten towns east of the river took their seats in the Assembly of Vermont, and it was proposed to erect a new county, to be composed of the towns which had been admitted to a union with Vermont; but this proposition was voted down, whereupon the members from the towns east of the river withdrew from the Assembly. Fifteen members from towns west of the river also withdrew, leaving just two thirds of the whole number, all of whom were required to be present for the transaction of business. The matter in relation to the union with New Hampshire was referred to the next Assembly.

Those who had withdrawn met in convention at Cornish, Dec. 9th, 1778, the towns on both sides of the river having been invited to send delegates. At this convention it was agreed to unite regardless of the boundaries established in 1764, and the convention also consented that the whole territory comprising the New Hampshire Grants might become one State as it was bounded previous to that time.— Until something of this kind should be accomplished, they resolved to trust in Providence and defend themselves. The propositions put forth by this convention were such, if adopted, as to unite a part of New Hampshire with a part of Vermont, or to destroy the government of Vermont and unite the whole territory with New Hampshire. Had a State been thus formed, the Capitol would undoubtedly have been located near Connecticut river; but this dangerous experiment was avoided in a singular way, without detriment to either State.

On the 12th day of February, 1779, the Assembly of Vermont voted to dissolve the union with the towns of New Hampshire. This unreliable course on the part of Vermont had the effect to encourage the authorities of New Hampshire, and cause them to claim the entire domain over which Wentworth exercised jurisdiction previous to 1764, and an application was made to Congress claiming the whole of Vermont. New York was awakened by these proceedings, and claimed the same territory.

At this time it began to look as though Vermont would be divided between New York and New Hampshire; and her condition was now more critical than at any previous period, for the reason that this controversy was a troublesome matter for Congress to deal with, and such a disposal of the territory of Vermont as was urged and expected by some, would destroy the State; but, if the entire matter of jurisdiction could be forever settled thereby, such a result did not seem to be then improbable.

Massachusetts also saw this glittering bait and put in her claim to a large portion of Vermont. Whether this was intentionally done on the part of Massachusetts to prevent the swallowing of Vermont in two parts, by two other states, or for some other purpose, is of but little consequence; but it may be justly said that Vermont owes Massachusetts a vote of thanks for that act. It was evident that something must be done forthwith, or civil war,

"The child of malice and revengeful hate,"

would cast its grim shadow over the territory in dispute, to the nation's peril.

The controversy with New York became intensified on account of the attachment of sundry influential persons, residing in Cumberland (now Windham) county, to that State, and their opposition to Vermont. They had boasted of their military strength, claiming that they had raised a regiment of 500 men who were opposed to Vermont and in favor of New York. Col. Ethan Allen was directed to engage a portion of the militia for the purpose of bringing these warlike demonstrations to a close, whereupon Col. Patterson of New York, sought the advice of Gov. Clinton as to holding the militia of Albany in readiness for any emergency, and suggested the propriety of employing the enemies of Vermont in each town as spies. The Governor became uneasy and wrote to the President of Congress, stating that he was daily expecting to order out a force to resist the troops commanded by Allen. On the 29th day of May, 1779, Congress referred the matter to a committee of the whole, and on the first day of June, by resolution, provision was made for a commission to settle all matters in dispute.

There were now four different claims submitted to Congress, to a tract of country, the inhabitants of which had been recently united under a Declaration of Independence, but were now at war with themselves and all the rest of mankind. On the 24th day of Sept., 1779, Congress passed a resolve recommending that New Hampshire, Massachusetts Bay, and New York, "forthwith pass laws expressly authorizing Congress to hear and determine all differences between them relative to their respective boundaries." It was also resolved that "in the opinion of Congress the three States aforementioned ought in the mean time to suspend executing their laws over any of the inhabitants of said district, except such of them as shall profess allegiance to, and confess the jurisdiction of the same respectively."

There being numerous persons in Vermont who adhered to all these States, this resolution, if carried out, would establish four governments over the people of Vermont. To have that number of separate jurisdictions operating at the same time over the same territory, after the people had assumed the functions of a State government, declared themselves free and independent, framed and adopted their constitution, enacted a code of laws and erected courts of justice, was a novel state of affairs from which no government outside of the New Hampshire Grants would ever expect to escape and be again identified by friend or foe.

On the second day of June, 1780, Congress passed a resolve declaring that the inhabitants of the New Hampshire Grants had pursued an unwarrantable course, subversive of the welfare of the United States and requiring them to exercise no further authority, civil or military, over those professing allegiance to the other states. To this resolution the Governor and Council made reply, asserting the independence of Vermont, and claiming that Congress had no right to meddle with their jurisdiction, as they were not included among the thirteen United States, but were at liberty to declare war or peace with Great Britain, without asking permission ; but so long as Congress declined to recognize Vermont in her independence, they had no interest to fight Great Britain for the purpose of defending a frontier for the benefit of the United States, but that they were willing once more to offer a union with the United States of America.

Congress seemed inclined to entertain this proposition, while New Hampshire and New York put in their claims that Vermont was not entitled to independence, but belonged to them. Vermont claimed a hearing, and was notified to appear on the 19th day of Sept., 1780, but her representatives were not allowed to be heard, whereupon on the 22d day of Sept. they filed a remonstrance to the proceedings as they were being carried on, and declared that if such was to be the manner of treatment on the part of Congress, they were "ready to appeal to God and the world, who must be accountable for the awful consequences that may ensue." The contending parties were so much exasperated as to suggest an alliance with Great Britain in case their rights were not respected. There was danger in this suggestion, but in order to obtain a decision in favor of Vermont, it was important to show that her military power would be of some value to the United States, and not be absorbed in contentions with other States. There was no time lost by either of the States in making reasonable and unreasonable efforts in their own behalf.

It was soon discovered that the inhabitants in most of the towns in western New Hampshire were desirous of being annexed to Vermont, who now proposed to take up the weapons used by her opponents, to wit, the claiming of jurisdiction. Thereupon a convention was held at Charlestown, N. H., Jan. 16th, 1781, and 43 towns in western New Hampshire were represented therein, a large majority being in favor of forming another union with Vermont; and a committee was appointed to consider the matter and report. On the 10th day of

February the assembly of Vermont, sitting at Windsor, received information from the committee that the convention of the New Hampshire towns "was desirous of being united with Vermont in one separate, independent government, upon such principles as should be mutually thought the most equitable and beneficial to the whole." On the 14th day of February, the Assembly of Vermont resolved to lay "a jurisdictional claim to all the lands whatever, east of Connecticut river north of Massachusetts, west of the Mason line and south of forty-five degrees north latitude." The convention of the New Hampshire towns, then in session at Cornish on the opposite side of the river, agreed upon a union on the 22d day of February; and the Assembly of Vermont resolved that the union, thus confirmed, should be held sacred. New York by this time began to discover that the frontier needed defence, and the inhabitants adjacent to Vermont petitioned the Assembly of that State for protection.

Upon this petition the Assembly of Vermont resolved to "lay a jurisdictional claim to all the land situate north of the north line of the state of Massachusetts, extending the same to Hudson's river; the east of the center of the deepest channel of said river, to the head thereof; from thence east of a north line, being extended to latitude 45 degrees; and south of the same line, including all the lands and waters to the place where this State exercises jurisdiction." In each of these unions jurisdiction

was not to be exercised for the time being; but petitions were soon received from the inhabitants of
New York praying that Vermont might exercise
jurisdiction without further delay. These last unions were more remarkable than any former effort in
that direction, being accomplished while New York
and New Hampshire were using every effort in their
power to extend their claims over the whole territory of Vermont.

When New Hampshire, New York and Massachusetts, were seeking to absorb the territory of Vermont, there was little or no sympathy manifested
for either state outside of its own limits; but when
Vermont turned the tables upon all of them, by lay-
ing claim to a large portion of New Hampshire and
New York, its policy, though aggressive, met with
so much favor that 35 towns in western New Hampshire and 10 districts in eastern New York, were
represented in the Assembly of Vermont, June 16th,
1781.

On the 20th day of August Congress passed a resolve setting forth that the people inhabiting the
territory called Vermont, as preliminary to their
admission into the federal union, should relinquish
all demands or claims of jurisdiction on the east side
of the west bank of Connecticut river, and also its
claim west of a line 20 miles east of Hudson's river.

In October the Assembly of Vermont convened at
Charlestown, N. H., and the resolve of Congress was
presented and rejected on the ground that it would

become necessary to break faith with New Hampshire in order to comply with the provision of Congress. Vermont, however, expressed a willingness to submit the boundary question to a commission.

New York became thoroughly frightened by the proceedings of Congress, and its Legislature claimed that that body had no right to intermeddle with matters of jurisdiction except in cases of dispute between two states already in the union, nor to admit even a British colony, except Canada, without the consent of nine states, nor to create a new state by dismembering one of the thirteen United States, without unanimous consent of the invaded state; and against all such procedure they entered a solemn protest. At this time Gov. Chittenden opened correspondence with Gen. Washington, claiming that Vermont had been driven to desperation by the injustice of those who should have been her friends. This correspondence was interrupted by the appearance of new and more threatening danger.

The Sheriff of a New Hampshire county which had been admitted to a union with Vermont, informed Gov. Chittenden that New Hampshire was preparing to compel those who had formed a union with Vermont, to conform to the authority of New Hampshire. While this excitement was at fever heat, the authorities of New York were trying to suppress what they called an insurection among the citizens who had united with Vermont. This new feature in public affairs made lively work for the inhabitants of the New Hampshire Grants, and at one time it looked as though Vermont might have its life squeezed out between New Hampshire and New York. They were all badly frightened at the prospect of civil war, but their relations with Great Britain furnished an outlet for their belligerent tendencies till better judgment overruled the passions of the hour.

The Commander-in-chief of the American army was much troubled by the contest between these states, and on the 1st day of January, 1782, he replied to Gov. Chittenden, advising Vermont to confine its jurisdiction to its old limits, and thereby obtain an acknowledgment of independence by virtue of the resolution of the 20th of August, 1781.

In February, 1782, the Assembly of Vermont met at Bennington, and the letter of Gen. Washington was there presented, and it was agreed to comply with his suggestion, whereupon the Assembly resolved. "That the foregoing recommendation be complied with, and that the west banks of Connecticut river, and a line beginning at the northwest corner of the State of Massachusetts; from thence northward twenty miles east of Hudson's river, as specified in the resolutions of Congress in August last, be considered as the east and west boundaries of this State. That this Assembly do hereby relinquish all claims and demands to, and rights of jurisdiction in and over any and every district of territory without said boundary lines."

The delicacy about encroaching upon the good faith of New Hampshire had been forgotten by Vermont, and the eastern union, which she had declared should be held sacred, was dissolved in a summary manner; and by a like process the western union was also terminated.

Vermont having thus complied with the resolves of Congress, proceeded to take measures for her admission into the union of states. The application was refused, and the people of Vermont began to suspect that Congress was not inclined to deal with them as had been intimated; but they continued to appoint agents to perfect arrangements for admission. Congress withdrew the continental troops, leaving the frontier exposed to the encroachments of the enemy. Vermont thus shorn of much of her political power, and essentially weakened in her means of defence, so long as she should exist outside of the Federal Government, still continued to assert her independence by declaring that she had as good a right to the same as Congress, and as much authority to pass resolutions prescribing measures to Congress as Congress had to give directions to her.

Some of the enemies of Vermont had been banished and their estates confiscated; and Congress demanded that full restoration should be made before the state could be admitted. New York was using every effort to keep Vermont out of the union, and the controversy between these three powers continued till October 28th, 1790, when the Assembly of Vermont, under advice of commissioners from both the states, agreed to pay $30,000 to New York in settlement of all matters between them in relation to boundary lines; and Vermont was admitted as a State, Feb. 18th, 1791., at which time all controversy with New Hampshire, New York and Massachusetts, was brought to a close.

Such has been the history of the unions, secessions and disunions of New Hampshire and Vermont, in early times. It may be easy to criticise New Hampshire for the part she took in furnishing material for this history. We may claim that Gov. Wentworth was a trespasser and a swindler; but if such was the fact, what shall we say of those who bought and paid for their lands in good faith, with a view to make themselves homes, establish institutions of learning, and receive further light in civilization? Are they to be censured for forming unions with a friendly ally, without reference to jurisdiction or boundary lines, when an unrelenting enemy with tomahawk and scalping knife in hand, stood ready to invade their peaceful firesides? If they met in secret conclave or open convention, resolving to do a work which they were unable to perform, are they to be looked upon with contempt for changing their course, their resolution, or their vote? Are they to be blamed for dissolving an unsatisfactory union and and forming another more complete and beneficial?

I might set forth in detail the action of the several towns on both sides of the river in relation to these unions, and delineate some of the scenes and personal encounters of those stirring times; but none of them, nor all combined, would change your opinion in relation to the honor and fidelity of the early patriots of New Hampshire. Without means of ready communication, liable to be surprised at any moment, day or night, by an uncivilized and dangerous foe, their willingness to unite with their friends and neighbors for the common defence was a virtue not to be despised; and the struggles they endured in behalf of their families, their homes and firesides, were not prompted by a spirit of invasion, nor the allurements of conquest.

After the dissolution of the eastern and western unions, in 1782, New Hampshire took but little interest in what transpired between New York and Vermont, or between both those states and Congress. This was not an unnatural course to pursue, for she had acquired an extensive territory not included in the grant to John Mason, which defined the actual territory of New Hampshire. Nor is there anything connected with the entire history of the New Hampshire Grants beyond the comprehension of an intelligent mind, or that could not be satisfactorially explained and accounted for, would time permit. Had New Hampshire been settled exclusively by the English as far west as the Connecticut river, Vermont by natives of Massachusetts and Connecticut, and New York by the Dutch, the unions, secessions and disunions, now seeming so peculiar to the local

historian, would never have occurred; and whoever
traces out the genealogy of the races who inhabited
this territory previous to 1780, will find a key to all
the strange problems with which the historian has
been perplexed.

It is true that the inhabitants of the New Hampshire Grants were a peculiar people. They were
adventurers, seeking homes in the wilderness, sur-
rounded by hostile and warlike tribes who sought to
overwhelm and destroy the unprotected colony.
They acknowledged no superior authority, except
God, the king, and the Continental Congress. They
enjoyed freedom of speech, an uncontaminated at-
mosphere, and plenty of hard work. They erected
their rude dwellings, churches and school houses,
subdued the forests, and planted the germ of a high-
er civilization. The sunlight that had gilded the
mountain tops through the lingering decades of unrecorded ages responded to the march of improve-
ment, and the valleys were made to blossom like
the rose. Their integrity, their honorable bearing
towards all men, their brave conduct in times of
peril, their fidelity to the most complete liberty of
mind and conscience, together with an unfaltering
faith in energy, perseverance and self reliance, made
them a terror to all tyrants, and champions of the
highest type of freedom.

No settlement was ever made on the habitable
globe by a more stern and conscientious race than
were the rustic pioneers who established their homes

within the jurisdiction of the New Hampshire Grants. Many of them had before been familiar with pioneer life, earning day by day their scanty meal and home-spun raiment,—destitute of every luxury except a clear conscience, and willing to spend their lives for the benefit of religious freedom, liberal education and good morals. They were quick to resent an injury, but ready to repair a wrong; and sometimes, with slight cause, they entered the arena of strife in behalf of state or country; and the daring deeds they performed at Ticonderoga and Bennington, give a peculiar charm to American history.

Whether they espoused the cause of New Hampshire, Vermont or Massachusetts, let the annals of a great empire continue to glow with the recorded valor of these illustrious men.